LC
Little Bunny

by Joanne Barkan
Illustrated by Jody Wheeler

Cartwheel
·B·O·O·K·S· ®

Scholastic Inc.
New York   Toronto   London   Auckland   Sydney

For Noa Bricklin,
baby of the year
—J.B.

For Jody Veet Wheeler,
teacher of the year
—J.W.

Hold each page of the book under a bright
light for a few minutes. Then turn out all the
lights, and see the pages glow! Once you have
"activated" the glow, you can use a flashlight
to recharge it.

Text copyright © 1995 by Joanne Barkan.
Illustrations copyright © 1995 by Jody Wheeler.
Published by Scholastic Inc. by arrangement with Brooke-House Publishing Co.,
25 W. 31st St., New York, NY 10001.

CARTWHEEL BOOKS is a registered trademark of Scholastic Inc.

Sparkle-Glow is a patent applied for process of Brooke-House Publishing Co.

ISBN 0-590-48932-1

12 11 10 9 8 7 6 5 4 3 2 1   5 6 7 8 9/9 0/0

Printed in the U.S.A.
First Scholastic printing, February 1995

"Snack time!" Mother Rabbit called from the vegetable garden.

Her bunnies lined up for their carrots.
"Here's one for Big Tooth," said Mother Rabbit.

"And one for Floppy Ear, and one for Puff Tail."
Suddenly Mother Rabbit looked worried.

"Where's Little Bunny?" she asked. "Is he hiding *again*?"

"I bet my big tooth he is," said Big Tooth.
"Let's look for him," said Puff Tail.

Hip-hopping and ears flopping, the rabbits raced to the dandelion meadow. They searched through the dandelions and grass.

"I don't see him," said Floppy Ear. "Do you?"

"Let's try the rocky field," said Big Tooth.
So off they ran.

"It's chock full of rocks here," said Puff Tail.
"But I can't find Little Bunny. Can you?"

Mother Rabbit sighed. "I don't think Little Bunny is hiding anymore. I think he's *lost*!"

"Oh, dear!" cried Floppy Ear. "He's lost! What should we do?"

"We'll search for him even harder," said Mother Rabbit. "Come along with me — and hurry!"

They dashed to the strawberry patch and shouted Little Bunny's name. But they couldn't find him.

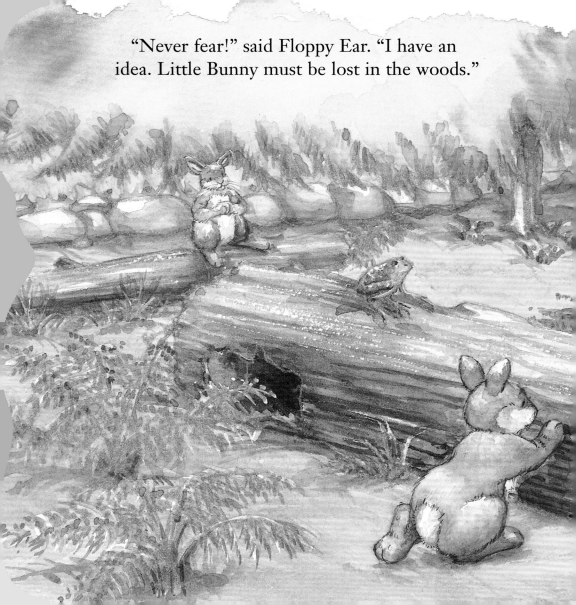

"Never fear!" said Floppy Ear. "I have an idea. Little Bunny must be lost in the woods."

The rabbits looked high and low in the woods. "There's no sign of him here," said Floppy Ear.

"I'll try the flower garden," called Puff Tail.
"Follow that Tail!" shouted Big Tooth.
The rabbits searched among the flowers. But they couldn't find even a whisker of Little Bunny's.

Big Tooth, Floppy Ear, and Puff Tail began to cry. Sad Mother Rabbit led them home to the vegetable

CABBAGE

EGGPLANT

garden. They walked slowly past the cabbage, eggplant, rhubarb, and peppers. And then —

"Do you see what I see?" asked Puff Tail.
Under the big carrot leaves lay Little Bunny.
Mother Rabbit's nose twitched happily. "He *was* hiding!" she said. "Now he's tired out and napping."

Can you guess what Mother Rabbit gave
Little Bunny when he woke up from his nap?
One big hug and his carrot snack!